W9-BFC-934

THE BEDTIME BEAST

Published by Raintree Publishers Limited Partnership

Library of Congress number: 89-3812

Library of Congress Cataloging in Publication Data

Hulbert, Jay.
The bedtime beast/Jay Hulbert; illustrated by Rowan Barnes-Murphy.

(Real readers)
Summary: Franny tells her grandmother that there's a beast in her room and it's keeping her from going to sleep.
[1. Bedtime – Fiction. 2. Stories in rhyme.] I. Barnes-Murphy, Rowan, ill. II. Title.
III. Series.
PZ8.3.H876Be 1989 [E] – dc19 89-3812
ISBN: 0-8172-3516-7

2 3 4 5 6 7 8 9 0 93 92 91 90

REAL READERS

The Bedtime Beast

by Jay Hulbert
illustrated by Rowan Barnes-Murphy

Raintree Publishers
Milwaukee

"It's bedtime now, Franny,"
Her grandmother said.
She kissed little Franny
And tucked her in bed.

But Franny soon ran down
The stairs with a ZOOM!
"I can't sleep," Franny said.
"There's a beast in my room!"

"Bedtime beasts will not hurt you,"
Her grandmother said.
"There's no beast in your room.
It is just in your head."

So Franny went back up
The stairs, but just then,
She heard an odd moan,
And she ran down again.

"Now it's singing!" yelled Franny.
"It sings out of tune!
If I go back to bed,
It may eat me—soon!"

"Just tell it to leave,"
Franny's grandmother said.
"Bedtime beasts will not eat you.
They are just in your head."

So Franny went up to
Her room, but one look,
And she saw that the beast
Was now eating her book!

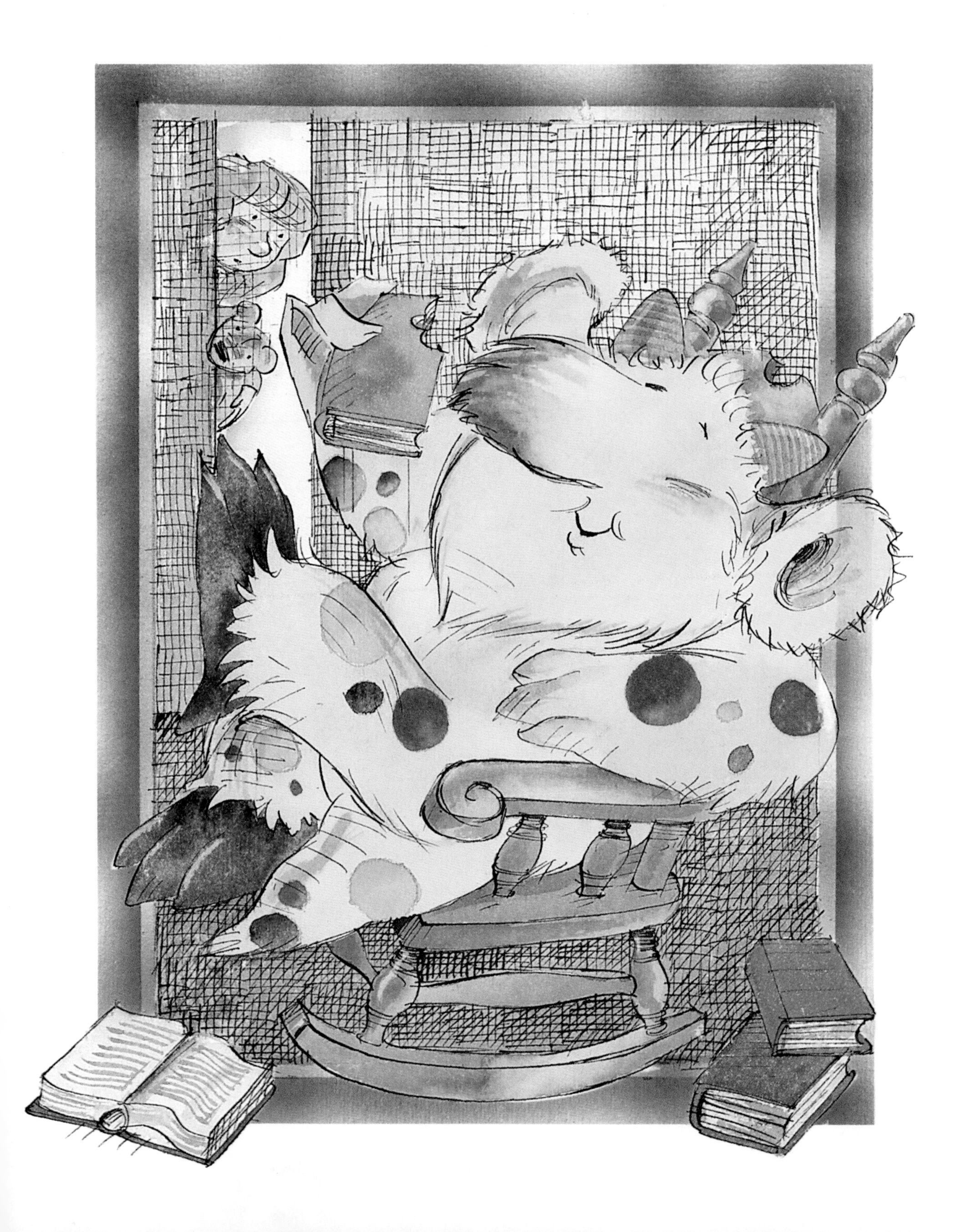

Franny yelled, "Bring up books!
Bring some books up, I say!
If we feed it some books,
Then it may go away!"

"Just tell it to leave,"
Franny's grandmother said.
"Bedtime beasts don't need books.
They are just in your head."

Franny looked at the beast.
She started to think.
Would that bedtime beast leave
If she gave it a drink?

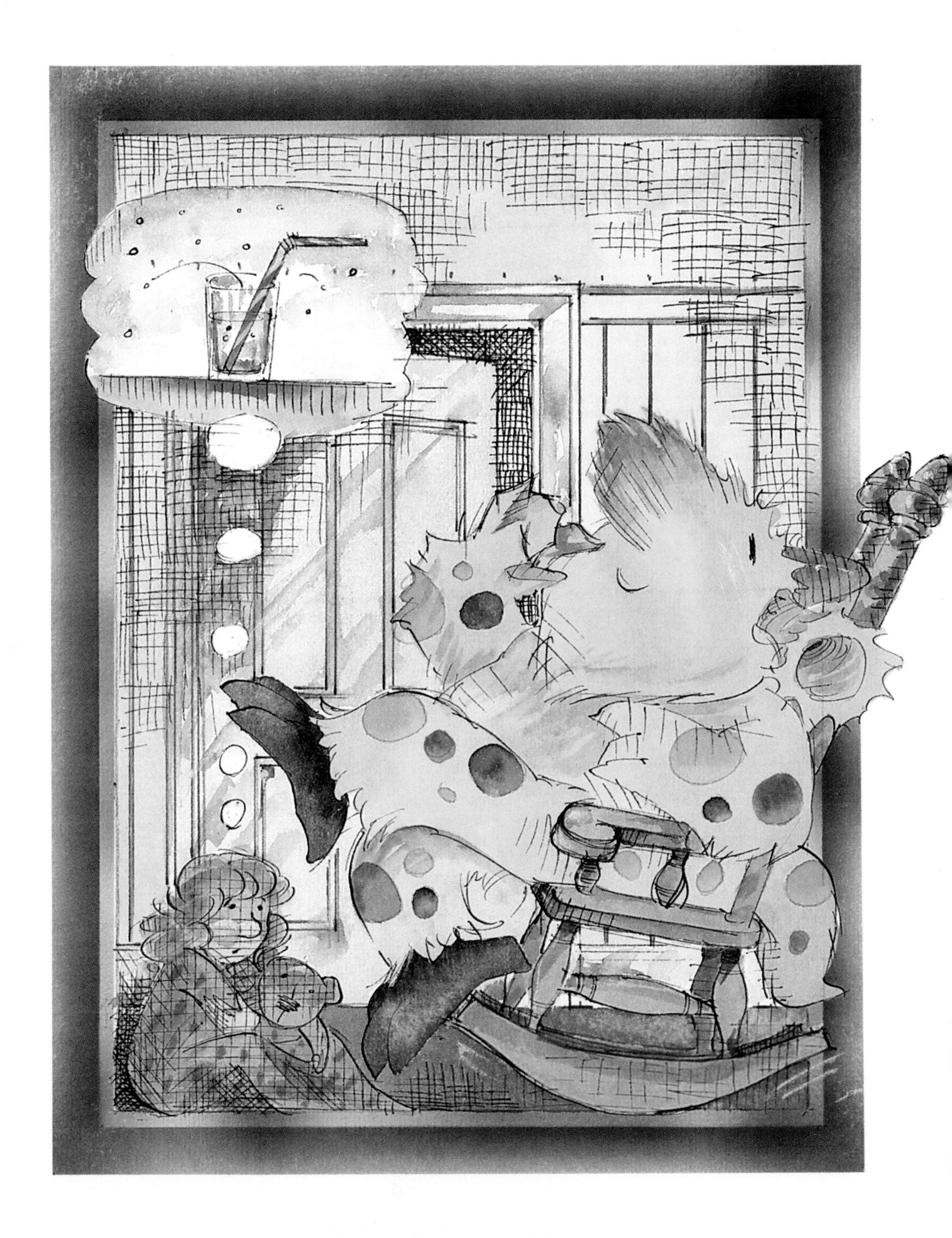

Franny went to Grandmother
And plucked at her sleeve.
"If the beast has a drink,"
Franny said, "it may leave."

"Just tell it to leave,"
Franny's grandmother said.
"Bedtime beasts do not drink.
They are just in your head."

Franny went to her room.
"Where's my drink?" the beast cried.
"I can't get one," said Franny.
"I'm sorry. I tried."

The beast was so mad
There was nothing to drink,
That it yelled and it cried,
Turning blue, green, and pink!

Franny ran downstairs fast,
And hid next to a plant.
"I will not go back up,"
Franny said, "I just can't."

"Don't be scared, little Franny,"
Her grandmother said.
"There's no beast in your room.
It is just in your head."

"Just tell it to leave,"
Said Grandmother, "Then
It will go to its home
And not come again."

"I know you can do it,"
Franny's grandmother said.
"I'll be up there soon.
Now, please, go to bed!"

So Franny went creeping
Up stair after stair.
When she got to her room,
The beast was still there.

The beast looked so mean,
It looked all set to stay,
But Franny went in
And she yelled, "GO AWAY!"

The beast's eyes filled with tears,
And it started to weep.
"I am sorry," said Franny.
"But I do have to sleep."

The beast cried and cried,
And it said with a moan,
"Please don't make me go,
I get scared all alone!"

Soon, Franny's grandmother
Came up as she said.
She went and kissed Franny
On top of the head.

And there on the rug,
She saw something new.
"It's a beast!" she said, shocked,
"And it's fast asleep, too!"

Sharing the Joy of Reading

Beginning readers enjoy reading books on their own. Reading a book is a worthwhile activity in and of itself for a young reader. However, a child's reading can be even more rewarding if it is shared. This sharing can enhance your child's appreciation— both of the book and of his or her own abilities.

Now that your child has read **The Bedtime Beast**, you can help extend your child's reading experience by encouraging him or her to:

- Retell the story or key concepts presented in this story in his or her own words. The retelling can be oral or written.
- Create a picture of a favorite character, event, or concept from this book.
- Express his or her own ideas and feelings about the characters in this book and other things the characters might do.

Here is an activity that you can do together to help extend your child's appreciation of this book: You and your child can make your own shadow beasts. You will need a room with only one source of light, either a lamp or a flashlight. Aim the light so that it shines on one wall of the room. Then you and your child can put your hands in front of the light so that the shadows fall on the wall. By moving your fingers, you can make different beast shapes. Try seeing how many different shapes you can make. Or, have conversations between the beasts by wiggling your fingers when you talk.